Another Rumpus!

Nick Ward

Albury Children's

Right in the **middle** of a scary monster sort of dream, Rumpus woke up. He woke up so suddenly that part of his dream stayed with him, and **crashing** into his bedroom came... Jamie.

"Help," cried Rumpus. "It's a horrid monster!"

"Don't be silly," said Jamie.

"It's only me!"

The boy and the monster had met before,
when the Rumpus had tumbled out of
Jamie's dream and into his bedroom.

You have
MONSTER
✉
Mail

"When you go to sleep,
I'll pop back into your dream,"
said Jamie. "Just like before."

Imagine the fright the monster Mom got when she saw Jamie!

"It's a horrid monster," she cried, diving under the kitchen table and upsetting the breakfast things.

"It's only my friend Jamie,"
said Rumpus. "He popped out of my dream
and wants to come to school with me."

So Mrs Rumpus made Jamie some breakfast...

... made him a packed lunch, and then walked the two friends to school.

Imagine the teacher's shock when Jamie walked into her class.

"Help, it's a horrid monster!"

yelled all the little monsters, sending paint pots and building bricks tumbling to the floor.

"It's only my friend Jamie," said Rumpus. "He wants to learn how to be a good little monster, **just like us!**"

First, the little monsters learned how to pull **horrible** faces.

The Brouhaha's was the **worst!**

← The Brouhaha

They made bloodcurdling noises.
The Hullabaloo was the best at this!

BLURGLE!

↑ The Hullabaloo

Then Teacher introduced a VERY SCARY
visitor to the class! Mr Rorty Snorty had come
to teach them how to be really SCARY monsters!

Mr Rorty Snorty waved his sharp yellow claws,
opened his big, toothy mouth, and roared like a terrible tornado.

"SCRAM!" he bellowed.

All the little monsters screamed, but Jamie took
a deep breath and roared right back...

NO, YOU SCRAM!

cried Mr Rorty Snorty, running away.
The frightened mega-monster didn't stop till he got home,
where he hid in a corner shaking and sucking his thumb.

"That was very good, Jamie," said Teacher.
"I think you deserve a prize for being the
SCARIEST MONSTER
EVER!"

He was very proud indeed, and Rumpus was very impressed.

After school, Jamie and Rumpus, Brouhaha and Hullabaloo played in Rumpus's garden.

But soon his friends started to get sleepy.
They were only little monsters, and it had been a very tiring day.
"We're pooped," they said, yawning.
"It's time for our nap."

"NO!" cried Jamie, but it was too late.
He popped right back into Rumpus's dream!

Far, far away in another world, Jamie woke up in the middle of a **scary** monster sort of dream.

He woke up so suddenly that part of his dream stayed with him, and crashing into his room came...

...a Rumpus, a Brouhaha
and a Hullabaloo!

For Lewis,
Aidan, Anthony and Ellis!
N.W.

First published in 2004 by Meadowside Children's Books,

This edition published in 2014 by Albury Books, Albury
Court, Albury, Thame, OX9 2LP, United Kingdom

Text © Nick Ward • Illustrations © Nick Ward
The rights of Nick Ward to be identified as the author and
illustrator have been asserted by them in accordance with
the Copyright, Designs and Patents Act, 1988

ISBN 978-1-909958-56-2 (hardback)
ISBN 978-1-909958-35-7 (paperback)

A CIP catalogue record for this
book is available from the British Library
10 9 8 7 6 5 4 3
Printed in China